I SURVIVED

THE BOMBING OF PEARL HARBOR, 1941

I SURVIVED

THE SINKING OF THE *TITANIC*, 1912

THE SHARK ATTACKS OF 1916

HURRICANE KATRINA, 2005

THE BOMBING OF PEARL HARBOR, 1941

I SURVIVED

THE BOMBING OF PEARL HARBOR, 1941

by Lauren Tarshis

illustrated by Scott Dawson

Scholastic Inc.

NEW YORK   TORONTO   LONDON   AUCKLAND
SYDNEY   MEXICO CITY   NEW DELHI   HONG KONG

ISBN 978-0-545-20698-3

Text copyright © 2011 by Lauren Tarshis
Illustrations copyright © 2011 by Scholastic Inc.
Photo on page 94 by Tim Hall
All rights reserved. Published by Scholastic Inc.
SCHOLASTIC and associated logos are trademarks and/or registered trademarks of Scholastic Inc.

47 46 45   19 20 21 22/0

Printed in the U.S.A.   40
First printing, September 2011
Designed by Tim Hall

FOR DYLAN

CHAPTER 1

DECEMBER 7, 1941
8:05 A.M.
PEARL CITY, HAWAII

America was under attack!

Hundreds of bomber planes were swarming over Pearl Harbor, Hawaii. They swooped down, machine guns roaring. Bombs and torpedoes rained down.

Explosions ripped through the blue Hawaiian sky.

Kaboom . . . Kaboom . . . KABOOM!

America's mightiest warships were in flames. A curtain of smoke — black and bloody red — surrounded the harbor.

Eleven-year-old Danny Crane had moved to Hawaii just weeks before. Ma had brought Danny to Hawaii to get him out of trouble, away from the crime and the rats and the dirty, dangerous streets of New York City.

But he'd never felt more terrified than he did right now, alone and running for his life. One of the attacking planes had burst out of the smoke and was closing in on him across an empty beach. Danny sprinted through the sand, but there was nowhere to go, nowhere to hide. He peered over his shoulder as the plane flew closer. He could see into the cockpit. The pilot was glaring at him through his goggles.

Rat, tat, tat, tat.

Rat tat tat tat.

Machine-gun fire!

Danny pushed himself to run faster. Searing pain filled his chest as he inhaled the smoky air.

Rat, tat, tat, tat.

Rat tat tat tat.

Sand flew up into Danny's eyes. And then from behind him, a huge explosion seemed to shatter the world.

The force lifted Danny off his feet and threw him onto the ground.

And then Danny couldn't hear anything at all.

CHAPTER 2

ONE DAY EARLIER
DECEMBER 6, 1941
PEARL CITY, HAWAII

Danny stood with his mother at the kitchen window of their tiny house.

Ma put her arm around Danny. "Just look at that view," she said. "Can you believe we live here? I think it's the most beautiful place on earth."

Ma was right; it looked like a postcard out there, with the palm trees swaying in the breeze, the bushes covered with pink and white flowers, and the ocean a sparkling silver strip in the distance.

Danny couldn't stand looking at it.

All he wanted was to be back in New York City, looking out his old apartment window at the jumble of dirty buildings, the smoke thick in the air, the garbage in the streets, and his best friend, Finn, waving to him from down in the alley below.

Ma thought that coming here to Hawaii would give Danny a fresh start. She wanted to get him away from danger and trouble, away from Earl Gasky and his gang.

It was true that Danny and Finn had gotten into trouble sometimes.

But nothing big! Just skipping school and sneaking into movie houses and nabbing an apple or two from the fruit stand.

Sure, they ran with Earl and his gang. Some folks in the neighborhood said Earl was a vicious criminal, that he'd break your legs if you looked at him wrong. But others said he and his guys protected the streets and took care of old ladies. He had always been good to Danny and Finn. He paid them a dollar a day to run errands. He even taught them how to drive one of his cars.

Sometimes it was scary, being on the streets so much, just Danny and Finn. But no matter what they were up to, they always looked out for each other.

Because who else was going to look after them?

Danny's father had been gone since before Danny was born. Ma did her best, but how could she watch over Danny when she was working all the time? She was so tired when she got home from her nursing shifts at the hospital. After kissing Danny hello, she would close her eyes for ten minutes, make their dinner, and then head out to clean offices until midnight.

And Finn's parents had five other kids crammed into a dark two-room apartment. So Danny and Finn stuck together, more than best friends, closer even than brothers. As long as they had each other, they felt like nothing bad could ever happen to them. And nothing ever did.

Until one night two months ago.

Even standing here, looking out on the palm trees, it all came back to Danny. It was like a horror movie playing in his mind. He could hear the screech of the metal on the fire escape breaking away from the building. He heard Finn's shout, and the thud of Finn's body hitting the sidewalk fifteen feet below. He could see Finn lying there on the sidewalk, the blood seeping out of his head, the flashing lights of the ambulance.

And then later, seeing him in that hospital bed, groaning in pain.

7

It was that night that Ma said they had to leave the city.

"It's time for us to go," Ma said. "Before something terrible happens to you."

When she first told him they were moving to Hawaii, Danny thought she was kidding. Wasn't Hawaii a made-up place, like Shangri-La?

But no.

It turned out it was a bunch of islands owned by America. There was a huge U.S. military base there called Pearl Harbor. They needed nurses at a hospital on an air base called Hickam. They wanted Ma right away.

A week later, the Cranes were on a train heading to San Francisco. From there, they took a ship halfway across the Pacific Ocean, to Oahu, one of the Hawaiian Islands.

Ma kept telling Danny how they needed to put New York behind them.

"We're starting out fresh," she said.

But how could Danny turn his back on Finn?

He couldn't, not when Finn needed him most. Besides, it was Danny's fault Finn got hurt. He was the one who wanted to climb up that fire escape, to explore that abandoned building on 23rd Street. Finn said it was a bad idea, but Danny told him to stop being a sissy. And then, as they were climbing up past the second floor, there was a terrible screech as the rusted metal of the fire escape gave way. Danny managed to climb onto the landing. But not Finn. He fell, crashing onto the cement sidewalk below.

And now Danny was an ocean — and a continent — away. But he had to go back to New York.

A ship called *Carmella* was steaming out of Honolulu Harbor tomorrow morning, heading back to the mainland.

Ma had no idea, but Danny was going to be on that ship.

CHAPTER 3

Ma straightened her white nurse's cap and kissed Danny good-bye. When she opened the door, Danny heard her gasp.

Danny hurried over. Ma said that there was no crime here in Pearl City. Still, Danny was used to being on the lookout for people lurking outside their door, waiting to pounce.

But there was nothing on their porch but a pot of pink flowers, wrapped in a bow.

"Goodness!" Ma said. "That man doesn't quit!"

Every morning for the past week, there had been a present waiting for Ma on their porch. They all came from a man named Lieutenant Andrew Maciel—Mack. He was a B-17 pilot at Hickam Air Force Base, where Ma worked. Danny had met him a few times when he drove Ma home. He came from New York City, so Danny figured he couldn't be all bad.

But then Danny found out he was from that fancy part of New York City called Sutton Place. Danny and Finn hated those rich Sutton Place kids, with their chauffeured cars and snooty expressions.

Danny hoped Ma wasn't sweet on this guy.

She smelled the flowers and smiled a little before handing the pot to Danny.

Then she kissed Danny again and headed on her way. Danny could hear her humming until she disappeared around the corner.

He brought the flowers to their little patio around back. He sat down on one of their rickety little chairs. The sun felt good on his face, and there was a warm breeze off the ocean. Maybe he'd miss the smell of the air here when he got back to New York — it smelled sweet, like sugar cane and pineapple. One thing he'd definitely miss was the sound of the bells that rang out every hour from the battleships anchored in Pearl Harbor.

The naval base was just five minutes from their house. There had to be a hundred warships crowded into the harbor with their guns ready to blast away. The best were the eight battleships. They were huge — like skyscrapers turned on their sides. Ma said the battleship guns were so powerful that one blast could blow an entire house to smithereens.

Danny wished he could tell his teacher in New York about those ships.

Most teachers at their school hadn't bothered

much with Danny and Finn. But Mrs. Mills was different. When it was too hot or cold outside, Danny and Finn would offer to wash Mrs. Mills's chalkboard for her. She always said yes, and she always happened to have a Thermos of lemonade or hot chocolate with just enough for them. She also had a big world map on the wall of her classroom. They could point to any country and Mrs. Mills could tell them everything about it.

More recently, Mrs. Mills had talked to them about the wars happening all around the world. She pointed to Asia, where Japan was fighting China. She pointed to Europe, where there was a maniac named Adolf Hitler in charge of Germany. He was sending his armies out to conquer every country he could.

Mrs. Mills hated Hitler.

"The world has to stop that monster," she told them. "He's marching across Europe now. But you watch. If we don't stop him, he'll want

America next. He'll want to hang a German flag over the Empire State Building."

Danny and Finn didn't like that idea one bit. And then one day they heard a shocking rumor: One of Earl's guys said that German U-boat submarines were sneaking around the waters just off Coney Island, in Brooklyn.

That did it! Danny and Finn skipped school

and hopped a subway down to Brooklyn. They sat there all day, freezing on Coney Island Beach, watching out for U-boats. They had no idea what a U-boat would look like. But that didn't matter. Finn brought his baseball bat. If a German soldier had tried to step onto the sand, Finn was ready to clobber him.

They didn't spot a U-boat. But the day wasn't a total waste. When Mrs. Mills heard that they'd skipped school to protect America, she gave them both an automatic 100 percent on their spelling tests. Finn grinned so big you could see the gold tooth from when he broke up a fight between two of his little brothers.

Thinking about his good times with Finn gave Danny a strange feeling. Of course Danny never cried — he was no sissy. And he'd learned a trick when he was younger. On those nights when he was alone in the apartment, wishing Ma wasn't gone so much, wondering why his father had left them, he'd push all the feelings down, and then pack them tight together. He could almost imagine them somewhere deep inside him, a hard ball of ice. Lately that cold hard place had grown so big Danny almost felt numb. But it was better than lying around crying.

Now Danny stood up, cursing himself for wasting time. He had to pack, write his note to Ma, get himself ready for the long journey back to New York City, to Finn.

But then he heard a commotion in his backyard.

There was a crash, a strange squeal, and an earsplitting scream.

CHAPTER 4

Danny flung open the back door.

Ma's new pot of flowers lay shattered on the ground.

Was someone in trouble?

Or were robbers planning to break in?

Danny picked up a broom, ready to strike.

The yard was small, just a patch of grass surrounded by a tangle of bushes and palm trees. He didn't see anyone, but then he caught sight of a small dark head poking out from behind one of the thick bushes.

Danny put down the broom and walked over. It was a little kid, maybe three years old.

What the heck was he doing here all by himself?

"Ahhhhhhhhhh!" the kid screamed.

Was the kid hurt?

"Hey!" Danny said.

The kid turned around.

He was grinning like a monkey standing on a mountain of bananas. And he was clutching a little animal of some kind.

"Puppy!" the kid said.

Danny studied the animal. It was very small and black except for one white ear.

He didn't want to break the kid's heart, but he was pretty sure it wasn't a puppy. It looked more like a rat.

"My puppy!" the kid said, hugging the poor

ugly critter so tight Danny was sure it would pop like a balloon.

Danny looked around. The kid was too young to be wandering around on his own.

"Who are you?" Danny said, bending down to look the kid in the eye.

"Aki!" he said. "Who you?"

"I'm Danny," said Danny.

"Danny see my puppy?"

Aki held out his poor squished pet like he wanted Danny to give it a big smooch.

And then the kid's eyes got huge. He pointed to something over Danny's shoulder.

"Monster!" he said.

Danny spun around and there, moving toward them, was the ugliest animal Danny had ever seen in his life. It was black, the size of a huge dog, with wiry bristles, a pig's snout, and two huge spiked tusks sprouting right from its face like swords.

It *did* look like a monster.

The animal grunted and snorted as it stared at Aki with beady black eyes.

Prepare to die! it seemed to be saying.

"Put down the puppy!" Danny said, suddenly understanding: That was a mother monster, and she thought Aki was stealing her baby.

"My puppy!" Aki screamed.

Danny pried the baby out of Aki's sticky hands. He gently placed it on the ground. The mother rushed up to it, nudged it with her nose, and gave a loud squeal.

"Okay," he said, bending down and speaking softly to Aki. "Let's go."

Aki screamed again, right into Danny's ear.

"My puppy!" Aki howled, lunging over to reclaim his pet.

The mother monster gave out a high-pitched roar.

Aki screamed right back.

This kid really was crazy!

Danny tried to grab Aki, but he pulled away.

The animal charged, its sharp tusks aimed right for Aki's stomach.

CHAPTER 5

Danny managed to grab Aki by the seat of his pants and hoist him up just in time.

One of the monster's tusks tore through Danny's pant leg. Amazingly, it missed his flesh.

Danny jerked back his leg, ripping his pants away from the tusk. He almost fell, but he regained his balance and kept his hold on Aki, who was still screaming for his puppy.

With Aki held high, Danny ran across the yard and into the house, slamming the door.

"My puppy!" Aki screamed. "My puppy!"

"No," Danny said, putting the kid down and blocking the door. "That's not yours. That's the monster's baby."

"Not Aki's puppy?" Aki said, his eyes getting bigger. There were tears now.

"Sorry, little guy," Danny said. "But that puppy has to be with its ma."

"Aki want puppy," he said, throwing his arms around Danny and burying his face in Danny's legs.

This kid was a stitch. Danny had always wanted a little brother, someone to trail along with him and Finn, someone to keep him company when Ma was working.

"Where's your ma?" Danny said.

"Mama mad at Aki," Aki said.

And sure enough, just then Danny heard someone shouting Aki's name.

Danny stuck his head out the window.

"I got him!" he called.

A moment later, he and Aki were standing on the porch with Aki's mother.

Danny guessed she and Aki were Japanese. There were people from all over the world living here — just like in New York City. Lots of the people in Pearl City were originally from Japan, Ma had said.

"Aki!" his mother scolded. "You cannot be running away like this!"

"I sorry, Mama," he said in a voice sweeter than a chocolate doughnut. He wrapped his arms around his mother's legs and gazed up at her with an angelic smile.

Danny saw how the anger in Aki's mother's eyes melted away.

This little kid was *good*.

She looked at Danny and smiled. Even though she looked nothing like Mrs. Mills, there was something about her that reminded Danny of his teacher — a look in her eyes, like she could read his mind and liked what she saw.

"Thank you," she said. "My son is a wanderer. The minute I turn my back, he sneaks away."

"We saw monster!" Aki said.

"A monster?" the woman said, raising her eyebrows.

"It looked like a hairy pig," Danny said. "With horns."

"A wild boar?"

"Monster hurt Danny," Aki said, pointing to Danny's torn pants.

"Goodness!" Aki's mother said with surprise. "Did he really hurt you?"

"Just my pants," Danny said. He decided not to tell Aki's mother how the boar almost turned Aki into a shish kebab.

"But it's very unusual for a boar to attack," said Aki's mother.

"Aki got hold of one of its babies," Danny said.

"Puppy." Aki smiled. "My puppy!"

Aki's mother shook her head.

"Aki sees the beauty in everything," his mother said. "Even a wild boar. But one of these days, Aki, you're going to end up in big trouble."

"He's a good kid," Danny said, wanting to protect his new friend.

"I good boy!" Aki said, puffing out his chest.

Danny and Aki's mother looked at each other, and they both laughed.

The sound startled Danny. He hadn't laughed since the night Finn fell.

Aki stared at both of them, trying to see what was funny.

Then he grabbed Danny's hand and started pulling with all his might.

"Danny come!" Aki said. "Danny come over!"

Danny opened his mouth to say "no thank you." But Aki kept shouting, "Danny come!" and pulling on his hand, trying to haul him up the hill. For such a shrimp, the kid was a real muscleman.

"You might as well come," Aki's mother said. "I have lunch just about ready. And as you can see, my son doesn't take no for an answer."

CHAPTER 6

Before Danny really understood what was happening, Aki had dragged him up to their house, if you could call it a house. It was smaller than the Cranes' house and made of cement, with a metal roof. Still, there was something nice about it—the white flowers climbing up one of the walls, the neat vegetable garden planted in front. Aki's mother had introduced herself on the way up—she was Mrs. Sudo. She explained that Aki's father was a fisherman out on a three-day trip. He'd be back tomorrow afternoon.

Mrs. Sudo had Danny sit down at a little wooden table in front of the house. Aki scrambled onto his lap. He stayed there as Mrs. Sudo served lunch. The food was weird — bowls of rice with fish in a salty sauce — but not so bad, especially the bright orange fruit for dessert. It tasted sweet as a lollipop.

After they ate, Aki curled up on Danny's lap. Danny thought he would fall asleep, tuckered out by all of the excitement.

But then a formation of bomber planes flew over them. There were always military planes crisscrossing the skies above Pearl Harbor. There were army and navy airfields all around the harbor, not only Hickam, where Ma worked.

Aki leaped up.

"B-18!" he shrieked. A minute later, three more planes appeared.

"A-20!" he shouted.

And finally, "Danny! B-17! Flying Fortress! B-17 Aki's favorite plane!"

"Aki knows all the planes," Mrs. Sudo said, putting another plate of orange fruit in front of Danny. "Aki, why don't you show Danny your book?"

Aki hopped off Danny's lap and shot into the house. He reappeared a minute later and handed Danny a worn sketchbook. He grinned proudly as Danny opened it. Danny stared at the pages, each one filled with perfect drawings of bomber planes and warships.

"You drew these?" Danny said in amazement.

"My papa!" Aki said.

"My husband drew those," Mrs. Sudo explained. "When he's home, he takes Aki down to the docks. They'll sit there for hours."

"He's really good," Danny said.

"He's an artist." Danny could hear the pride in Mrs. Sudo's voice. "Fishing is just his job."

P-26
(MOSTLY TRAINER)

B17 BOMBER
"FLYING FORTRESS"

BELLY BALL
TURRET →

A20
"HAVOC"

P-40

B-18 BOMBER

"I wish I could draw," Danny said.

Actually he already could draw, a little bit. Mrs. Mills got him a sketchbook and told him to practice, but he never made much progress.

"My husband would love to help you learn," Mrs. Sudo said. "Is your father in the military?"

"No," Danny said. "It's just me and my ma. She works as a nurse at Hickam. We moved here from New York City a couple of weeks ago."

"Your mother's very brave, to come all this way to start a new life."

Danny had never really thought of it that way. Ma had looked so scared after Finn fell. But he guessed it was brave, to leave the city she'd lived in her whole life, to travel halfway around the world.

"She's lucky to have a boy like you," Mrs. Sudo said.

The words hung in the air a minute—*a boy like you*—and then they seemed to slap Danny in the face.

Tears came into Danny's eyes, but he had no idea why.

Somehow, being here with Aki and Mrs. Sudo, some of that ice inside him had melted.

He had to get out of here.

He stood up so quickly that he dropped Aki's book onto the floor.

"Thank you for lunch," he said, picking up the sketch pad and handing it to Aki. "But, uh, I have to go."

"Danny!" Aki shouted. "Stay!"

"You're welcome to stay the afternoon," Mrs. Sudo said. "Until your mother returns from work."

"I'm sorry," Danny said. "I'm sorry, but . . . I have to leave."

And without even a wave good-bye, he ran down the hill and into his house.

CHAPTER 7

THE NEXT MORNING
DECEMBER 7, 1941
8:05 A.M.

Danny lay in his bed, listening to the morning birds sing outside his window.

The *Carmella* was leaving in two hours. He was all ready for the trip. He had packed a small bag. He had written the note to leave for

Ma. And he had the entire plan laid out in his head.

Stowing away on the *Carmella* would be easy — one of Earl's guys did it once when he was younger: stowed away to Cuba to track down an old girlfriend. You had to be smart about it — dress nice, wash up, pretend you were visiting some passengers. Then, when the bell rang for all the visitors to leave, you had to find a good hiding place, like a storage closet, or a lifeboat, if you could sneak in without someone seeing you. Anywhere you could stay out of sight for at least a day, until the ship was far out to sea.

After that, if you got caught, there wasn't much the crew could do. They wouldn't toss Danny overboard. He'd already figured out his sob story: He was an orphan, trying to get back to New York to be with his cousin Finn. He might even mention the name Earl Gasky.

People had heard of Earl, even outside of New York. Danny heard that he was even friends with some guys in the FBI. Earl could get people to do all kinds of things, even give a kid a ride across the Pacific.

The trip would get trickier when the boat docked in San Francisco. Danny would have to slip away before the police got there. He'd have to get himself to the freight train yards. Riding freight cars wasn't so easy. Danny had heard bad stories about the "yard bulls," the guards who searched the sidings for train jumpers. They'd beat you up and then toss you through the doorway of the police station.

But none of this scared Danny.

So what was he doing still in bed?

He should have gone to the Honolulu port right after Ma left for work at 7:00.

But he couldn't bring himself to leave. All night, he'd been hearing Mrs. Sudo's voice in his head.

Your mother is lucky to have a boy like you.

A boy like Danny.

What kind of boy was he?

A boy who didn't turn his back on his best friend.

But did that mean he was a boy who would leave his ma?

All these weeks he'd been thinking about doing what was right for Finn, but now he couldn't stop thinking about Ma. What would she do when she discovered that Danny was gone? He couldn't even imagine it, how frantic she'd be.

All night he'd been tossing in his bed, feeling torn in two.

He was lying there, his thoughts seesawing back and forth, when a familiar voice rang out.

"Danny! Danny, come!"

Aki was outside again.

Now his plans would really be messed up!

Danny climbed out of bed. He quickly dressed

and went to the door. Aki was standing there by himself.

"Aki," he said. "What are you doing here?"

The kid wasn't wearing his crazy monkey grin. His face looked dead serious.

He pointed up to the sky and said in a soft and scared voice, "Airplanes."

CHAPTER 8

"Come on," Danny said, picking Aki up. "We need to get you back home. Your mama will be very worried."

"Airplanes," Aki said, looking into the sky.

"Aki, you have to go home, come on, you have to . . ."

Aki put his hand on Danny's mouth, silencing him.

"Shhh!" he said. "Airplanes."

Danny almost pulled Aki's sticky hand off his face.

But then he heard a sound he'd never heard before.

A buzzing sound, like there was a giant swarm of bees closing in.

Danny followed Aki's pointed finger. And then he saw it in the distance—what looked to be an enormous flock of gray birds flying toward Pearl Harbor.

As the gray spots grew larger, Danny could see that Aki was right. They were airplanes. More than Danny had ever seen. And then he saw even more, coming in from another direction.

There must be a drill going on. The navy and army were always practicing. There had been a drill at Hickam last week, when fifty sailors had to pretend to be wounded. Ma came home exhausted and covered in fake blood.

Whatever game these planes were playing, Danny didn't have time to watch them, not if

he planned to catch the *Carmella*. He'd already
wasted too much time bellyaching in bed.

"Come on," Danny said, holding out his hand.
If he hurried, he'd get Aki home and then be
able to hitchhike to Honolulu. He could still
make it to the port in time.

Then, when they were almost up the hill, an
enormous *BOOM* shook the ground.

And then another.

Danny stopped short.

"Fire!" Aki shouted.

Flames were rising from one of the battleships.

What kind of drill was this? Had a pilot crashed or dropped a bomb by mistake?

Danny stopped moving. Aki wrapped his arms around Danny's neck. Danny could feel the little boy's heart beating, like tiny running footsteps.

Together they stared at the scene over the harbor.

The planes were flying so low they seemed to skim the tops of the taller ships.

Kaboom!

Another explosion rang out.

Sirens began to howl.

Boom . . . boom . . . BOOM . . . BOOM!

The sky was filling with black smoke.

"My ships," Aki whispered.

A feeling of dread came up through Danny, a black and swirling feeling, like on that night with Finn, when he'd first heard the metal of the fire escape start to give way. He knew something horrible was happening, something beyond his worst nightmares.

He gripped Aki tighter.

"Aki," Danny said. "Are those B-17s?"

Aki shook his head.

"Are they B-18s?"

Again Aki shook his head.

"A-20s?"

"Not Aki's planes."

And that's when Danny knew.

It was Hitler! Germany was attacking! Just like Mrs. Mills had said it would!

More explosions rang out. The air filled up with a horrible smell.

A voice rang out.

"Aki!"

Mrs. Sudo came running down the hill.

"Thank goodness!" she cried, grabbing Aki and hugging him.

"The Germans are attacking us," Danny said.

Mrs. Sudo turned to Danny.

She had tears in her eyes.

"No, Danny," she said. "Those are not Germany's planes."

"Who else could it be?" Danny said. Who else was crazy enough to bomb Pearl Harbor?

"Those are Japanese planes," Mrs. Sudo said.

Japan?

What had America done to Japan?

Why would they want to destroy all of those ships?

There were no answers, just more explosions, more of that black, bloody-looking smoke.

Aki was crying.

"Come," Mrs. Sudo said, grabbing Danny's hand. "I know somewhere we can go, in case . . ."

Danny knew what she wasn't saying: *In case the planes started bombing their houses too.*

They hurried up and around the back of the Sudos' little house. Danny helped Mrs. Sudo open the wooden door that led to her root cellar — not much more than a hole in the dirt. Mrs. Sudo went down the narrow wooden stairs first, and Danny handed Aki to her.

"Come, Danny," Mrs. Sudo said.

But Danny was staring out over the smoke and flames.

Somewhere in the middle of all that was Hickam.

And somewhere at Hickam was Ma.

"I need to find my mother," he said.

"No! Your mother would want you here! Please stay! She would want you to be safe!"

Danny knew that was true.

But he ran away anyway, down the hill, toward the fires, toward Ma.

CHAPTER 9

As Danny hurried past his house, he barely recognized his new neighborhood.

Cars sped by. People were running through the streets, shouting. A truck rumbled past with a man hanging out the passenger window. He was yelling through a bullhorn.

"All military personnel! Report to your posts! We are under attack! We are under attack! This is not a drill! America is under attack by Japan!"

Military men were rushing out of their front

doors, buttoning their uniform shirts as they ran, calling out good-byes to their wives and children.

"Take the kids up to the cane fields!" one yelled. "Hide if you have to! I'll find you when this is over!"

Some of the ladies stood in the doorways and cried.

Danny ran across the street to the beach. Through a curtain of smoke across the harbor, Danny could see the planes pummeling the battleships, flying low, firing their guns, and then circling back for another attack.

The noises pounded in Danny's ears.

Boom. Boom. Boom. BOOM!

Rat, tat, tat, tat.

Keeeee POW!

Where was Ma?

Was she safe in the hospital, or were the Japanese trying to blow that up too?

How would he get to her?

Tears came into Danny's eyes.

And then suddenly something appeared through the smoke. One of the planes had peeled away and was heading his way.

Danny expected it to loop around and head back to the harbor.

But it was coming toward the beach.

Straight for Danny.

Danny stood there, frozen by fear. He watched as the plane got closer and closer, until he could see the pilot. The man looked very young. He had a white rag tied around his head. He wore goggles. His plane had big red circles on both sides.

Danny remembered Mrs. Mills's classroom. She had pictures of all the flags of the world lined up. Japan's was a white flag with a red ball in the middle.

The red ball was supposed to be the rising sun, Mrs. Mills said.

But now all Danny could think of was a ball of fire.

There was a terrible roaring sound.

Rat, tat, tat, tat.

Rat tat tat tat.

Sand flew up all around Danny. Machine-gun fire! Why was the pilot shooting at Danny?

Danny ran across the sand. But there was nowhere to hide.

The roar of the plane got louder as Danny ran.

Rat, tat, tat, tat.

Rat tat tat tat.

Behind him, there was an explosion so enormous that the ground beneath Danny seemed to rise up.

His head smashed against the sand.

And then he couldn't see anything at all.

CHAPTER 10

8:45 A.M.

Danny wasn't dead.

His head felt like it had been split in two.

His hands and knees throbbed.

His mind swirled.

His mouth was filled with sand and blood; he'd bitten his tongue. His ears were ringing.

But he was all in one piece.

He had no idea how much time had passed since that plane appeared.

The plane was gone now. The attack seemed to be over.

As his mind cleared, he managed to sit up. Over the harbor, one of the battleships was a ball of fire. That was the huge explosion: An entire battleship had been blown apart.

That's what had knocked him down.

Danny finally struggled to his feet and staggered across the beach toward the road.

He saw a car parked at the edge of the beach, the front end partially hidden in a prickly bush. It was covered with bullet holes. The back window was shattered. He didn't see anyone; probably the driver had run away. Danny wondered if the guy would mind if he borrowed it. Earl had not only taught Danny and Finn how to drive. He'd shared a secret for starting a car engine without a key.

But as Danny got closer to the car, a man's

face appeared through the shattered driver's window.

"Hey, kid," he called. "You okay?"

Danny couldn't believe his eyes. It was his mother's friend, Mack.

"Dan!" Mack said. "Is that really you? Are you okay? Were you hit?"

"I'm okay," Danny said.

"Where is your mother?" Mack asked.

"She's at the hospital," Danny said, his voice shaky. "At the base. I think it was hit. I need to get there."

Mack looked nothing like a fancy Sutton Place man trying to impress Danny's mother. His expression was fierce and determined.

"Let's go," he said. "That's where I'm heading. You come with me. We'll find her."

When Danny got into the car, he noticed blood spattered on the doors. Mack's arm was bleeding badly.

"You're hurt," Danny said.

Mack glanced at his arm. "I got grazed by a bullet," he said. "I've had worse."

He pulled the car up onto the road and they drove off.

"They caught us by surprise," Mack said. "The Japanese blindsided us."

"Why?" Danny said.

"To knock out our ships and bombers," Mack said. "To cripple our entire Pacific fleet. That way they can take over whatever they want in the Pacific — China, the Philippines, Korea. Japan is a small country, but they want to be powerful. They need more land. So they're taking over other countries, like Hitler has been doing in Europe. And now we won't be able to stop them."

"But didn't we know they would do this?" Danny said. "Shouldn't we have known?"

"Some people talked about it," Mack said. "But nobody thought they could pull it off."

Mack looked at Danny.

56

"I'll tell you what," he said. "The Japanese made a mistake. A big mistake. They have no idea what they've started. This country is going to rise up and crush them. You'll see."

"And what about Hitler?" Danny said.

"Him too," Mack said.

Mack sounded so sure. And Danny wanted to believe him. But now he was thinking about Mrs. Mills's map, stretched across the classroom wall. How could America fight two wars on opposite sides of the world?

As Hickam came into view, Danny could see smoke and flames rising from the base.

Mack swore under his breath.

They pulled up to the gate, which was blocked by a smashed car, still smoldering.

"Let's go," Mack said, opening his door.

Danny followed Mack around the burning car and toward the gates at the base.

Ahead, the base reminded Danny of a photo he'd seen in *Life* magazine of a town that had been hit by a tornado. There was wreckage everywhere — twisted metal all over the ground, shattered glass, pieces of burned wood. He stepped over a tattered hat. He wondered what had happened to the man who'd been wearing it.

Some of the buildings had been destroyed; two were still burning. The air was hard to breathe. It smelled like burned rubber and plastic. And everywhere he looked, Danny saw wrecked planes. Some were cut right in half.

Two armed guards stood at the gate. They both saluted when they saw Mack, and then they both started talking at once.

"We were hit bad, sir!"

"We've lost about a dozen men, sir!"

"About a hundred are wounded."

"They destroyed the barracks and the mess hall. Two hangars are gone."

"We lost a lot of planes, sir. They torched them right on the runways."

Mack listened closely to the rush of information. Finally he held up his hand to quiet the men.

"Did we get any planes into the sky?" Mack asked.

"No, sir."

"Hospital okay?" Mack said, reading Danny's mind.

"Hospital's fine, sir. No hits. They're treating the wounded."

Danny closed his eyes with relief. And then he heard a ferocious roar.

Another wave of Japanese bomber planes roared out of the sky, whistling through the smoke, right over their heads.

Bombs started pouring down.

CHAPTER 11

In an instant, a bomb exploded on the runway. A man disappeared in a blaze of flames and black smoke.

Danny and Mack and both guards hit the ground hard.

Mack came over and shielded Danny's head and shoulders with his body. He waited for a lull in the explosions and then he scrambled to his feet. He grabbed Danny's hand, yanking him up.

"We need to get out of here!" he shouted to the guards. "We need to find cover!"

Turning to Danny, Mack yelled, "Come on!" Mack held Danny's hand tight as they ran. "Keep your head down!"

But where could they go?

Bombs were exploding all around them.

Boom! A truck exploded.

Boom! Three men fell to the ground.

A plane flew in low.

Pom, pom, pom, pom, pom.

A spray of bullets ripped apart a car.

Soldiers were crouched behind bushes and under cars. Some had small handguns and were firing uselessly into the sky. One soldier threw rocks. Danny couldn't believe it; did they really think that would stop the planes?

But he understood too. There was nothing they could do.

Mack dragged Danny behind what was left of a huge airplane hangar. Through the enormous holes in the walls, Danny saw U.S. bomber planes—shattered and burning. In the lawn behind the hangars, bombs had blown craters into the grass. Mack pushed Danny into one and then jumped in after him.

"Get down!" Mack said.

Danny curled up against the dirt wall, and Mack crouched next to him, shielding Danny with his body.

Men shouted all around them.

"He's hit!"

"Watch out!"

"We need help!"

"They're coming in low!"

Danny pressed his head against the side of the hole. Mack held him tight.

"It will be over soon!" Mack said.

But the planes kept coming. Danny peered up, knowing he'd never forget the sight of those planes. They were small and gray, like killer birds.

A whistling sound cut though the air, and then —

Kaboom!

Dirt, rocks, and metal rained down on them. Something sharp stabbed Danny in the calf. He reached around and pulled out a small piece of metal, tossing it behind him.

Danny closed his eyes tight, praying for the attack to stop.

Suddenly he thought of Finn. He could almost feel that Finn was with him there, telling him to be brave. The feeling was so powerful — it filled Danny's entire body.

And finally the thundering stopped.

The attack was over. The roar of the planes was replaced by the shouts of men.

Danny turned, and Mack fell back, his eyes dazed.

"I'm hit," he rasped. "My back. I think it's bad."

Danny looked at Mack's back. His stomach

heaved as he saw a jagged wound. And more blood than he had ever seen.

Mack wouldn't last long, bleeding like this.

A blond soldier appeared above the crater. His glasses were cracked and he had a gash on his face.

"Everyone all right here?" he asked.

"He's bleeding bad, sir!" Danny said.

The soldier shouted for help, and within seconds he and another man were helping Danny lift Mack from the crater. Mack winced in pain as they pulled him onto the grass and laid him on his side. The soldier pressed against the wound with his bare hand, trying to slow the bleeding.

"Hang on, sir," the blond soldier said. "Help is on the way."

But Danny didn't see any help.

"Are there ambulances?" Mack asked.

"All the ambulances are out, sir."

Mack nodded grimly. His jaw was clenched and his face was very pale.

"What about that car?" Danny asked, pointing to a red Studebaker parked next to the hangar.

"That belongs to our colonel," the soldier said.

Danny leaped up and rushed to the car.

"Wait!" the soldier shouted.

But Danny ignored him.

The car had been spared any hits. It barely even had a scratch.

Danny lifted the hood and studied the engine. He easily found the two ignition wires Earl had shown him.

"You never know when you need to get somewhere quick," Earl had said with a smile.

As usual, Earl had been right.

Danny carefully touched the wires together. The engine sputtered to life.

Danny flung open the door and jumped inside. He drove the car around holes and chunks of glass and metal, pulling up as close as possible to where Mack lay.

The blond soldier looked worried. But Mack managed a smile.

"Good work, kid," he said. "I won't ask where you learned how to do that. But I'm darned glad you did."

Danny and the soldier helped Mack into the car.

"Go!" the blond soldier said. "The hospital is half a mile down, on the right."

"Wait," Mack said. "There are other guys who need help. We're not leaving until the car is full."

Five minutes later, there were two more wounded men in the car. One man had so much blood on his face that Danny couldn't tell what he looked like. The other was holding on to his leg like it might fall off.

Danny drove as fast as he could to the hospital. The road was cratered and filled with burned wreckage. Once he had to get out and drag a huge piece of a plane out of the road. But finally he made it.

When they got to the hospital entrance, Danny blared the horn, signaling for help.

While they waited for help, Danny turned and looked at Mack.

Mack's eyes were fluttering. Danny wasn't sure what to do. And then he reached over and grabbed Mack's hand.

"Mack," he said.

"What?" Mack rasped.

He could only think of one thing to say.

"I'll make my ma have dinner with you," Danny said. "When you get better."

Danny saw a flicker of a smile cross Mack's face. Outside the car, two orderlies rushed out with a stretcher.

Behind them were two nurses.

One of them was Ma.

CHAPTER 12

The next twenty-four hours rushed by in a blur of sirens and blood and moaning, shouting men. But Danny barely had time to think about any of it. He was too busy.

After that first moment when he and Ma saw each other — Ma hugged Danny so tight she almost cracked his ribs, and he hugged her back even tighter — she put Danny to work in the hospital. Hundreds of Hickam men had been wounded. They were the lucky ones. Dozens had died when a bomb destroyed the barracks while men were just waking up. Dozens more never made it out of the dining hall when a bomb set it on fire. Others had been hit on runways, in hangars, or while firing machine guns at the bombers.

There were only two doctors and two nurses at Hickam. They needed every spare hand they could find.

Danny helped soldiers and volunteers make beds and sweep glass off the floor. He rolled bandages and found extra blankets for men recovering from surgery. He watched Ma as she hurried from man to man, changing bandages, holding hands, never flinching. Mrs. Sudo was right—she was brave. A few times Danny managed to peep in on Mack. Ma said he'd been given a powerful drug to take away the pain. He'd lost almost half of his blood. But Ma said he'd survive.

As bad as things were at Hickam, Danny

knew they were even worse out on the harbor. All night reports trickled in: The battleship *Arizona* was gone, along with more than a thousand men. The *Oklahoma* was capsized, and more than a hundred men were still trapped inside. The *California* was sinking. The destroyers *Shaw* and *Cassin* had exploded. Other ships were badly damaged. For most of the day, Pearl Harbor was a sea of fire. Even men who managed to escape the burning ships had little chance of survival. Hundreds of planes at different bases had been destroyed or badly damaged. Hospitals all over Oahu were overflowing with wounded men. Danny heard that his school had been turned into a hospital.

Everyone expected another attack. There were whispers about a Japanese invasion of Hawaii. Danny tried not to think about this, about how easy it would be for the Japanese to take over the island with so many ships and planes wrecked.

The hours ticked by with no more Japanese planes.

But America was now at war. Danny knew it would be months or even years before the sound of a plane in the sky didn't make him jump.

It wasn't until the next morning that Ma and Danny finally got to sit together. Ma slumped in her chair, more tired than Danny had ever seen her. Her white uniform was spattered with blood. But she listened closely as Danny told her the story of how he had been with Aki when he saw the first planes.

Ma told him about the terrifying first minutes when the bombs started dropping on Hickam.

"We'll remember this moment for the rest of our lives," Ma said.

Then she let out a strange sigh. "To think, I got you out of New York because I wanted you in a safe place."

She shook her head, and Danny could see she was fighting back tears.

"I'm glad we're here."

The words came out before Danny realized what he was saying. And Ma liked hearing them. She smiled a little.

Just then, one of the doctors peeked his head in and said he needed Ma for surgery.

"See you soon," she said to Danny as she headed out the door. "Don't go away, okay?"

She was joking, Danny knew. Because where could he go from here?

But he thought with shame of his plan to leave on the *Carmella*.

Would he really have gone?

If those planes hadn't attacked today, would Danny be on that ship?

He couldn't say.

It seemed impossible that only twenty-four hours had passed since he first saw those planes. Because everything seemed completely different now. Not just the harbor, now in ruins. Not just America, now at war.

But Danny too.

Maybe yesterday morning he had been the kind of boy who would leave his ma. He would never know for sure.

But he knew this: He wasn't that kind of boy anymore.

CHAPTER 13

DECEMBER 9, 1941
9:00 A.M.

It was two long days before Ma and Danny left Hickam.

The first thing Danny did was change his clothes. The next thing he did was sprint up to the Sudos' house.

Aki ran to him.

Danny had brought him a present — one of
the airmen had given Danny his wings.

Danny clipped the gold pin onto Aki's shirt.

"Mama!" Aki shrieked. "Look!"

Mrs. Sudo stepped away from her clothesline.

She smiled at Danny and hugged him.

But Danny noticed her red and swollen eyes.

A feeling of dread came over Danny.

He saw no sign of Mr. Sudo.

Mrs. Sudo had Danny sit down at the little table where they'd had lunch just a few days ago. She sent Aki into the house to get his toy trains.

And she told Danny what had happened. Somehow, Mr. Sudo had made it home from fishing the night after the attack. But the next day, the police had come to the house.

They were searching the houses of all Japanese people in Hawaii.

Mrs. Sudo looked down. "They are looking for spies."

"Spies?" Danny asked.

"They said that local Japanese here had helped with the attack. They asked if they could search our home, and of course we said yes. Because there is nothing here we have to hide."

Mrs. Sudo pushed her lips together and took a ragged breath.

"But they did find something. Something they said proved that Aki's father was helping the Japanese. The sketchbook. With all of his drawings of ships and planes. They took it. And then they took my husband to jail."

Danny tried to understand what Mrs. Sudo was saying.

"What's wrong with drawing the ships and planes?" Danny said.

"They said he had given information to the Japanese about what ships were in the harbor, and what kind of planes we had. They said he helped them plan the attack."

"But didn't you tell them that's not true?"

"Of course we did, Danny. My husband has lived in Hawaii his whole life. He loves America. This attack enraged him. That night he came home from fishing, he said he wanted to join the navy—the U.S. Navy—and fight the people who did this to our beautiful Hawaii."

"Did you tell them that?"

"Of course," Mrs. Sudo said. "But they didn't listen. I heard they have arrested other Japanese people. There is a rumor that they are going to put all Japanese people in America in jail."

Danny couldn't believe that was true. Mrs. Mills always said America was the land of the free.

Just then, Aki came running out with his toy train.

"Danny play!" he said.

Mrs. Sudo patted Danny's hand and got up to finish the laundry. Probably the best thing he could do for Mrs. Sudo was to keep Aki busy.

And so he brought Aki back to his house and they spent the afternoon playing.

All that afternoon Danny thought about Mr. Sudo.

Was there any way he could help?

Nothing came to him.

Until later that night, when he was lying in bed.

Danny realized that there was one person who might be able to do something.

And the next morning, he went to the post office and sent a telegram to Earl Gasky.

There was no way of knowing whether Earl had anything to do with Mr. Sudo's release from jail a week later.

But Danny knew that Mr. Sudo was back, because he heard a shriek from the hill.

"Papa!"

An hour later, Aki had dragged Mr. Sudo down to meet Danny.

Of course Danny didn't mention to Mr. Sudo that he'd asked a gangster to help free him from prison. Who knew if the telegram had ever reached Earl. And if it had, who knew if Earl had even cared.

But right now there wasn't much Danny could believe in. So he decided to believe in Earl.

CHAPTER 14

DECEMBER 25, 1941
7:30 A.M.

On Christmas morning, Danny was awakened by a strange noise.

He sat up in bed, wide awake, wondering if he needed to wake up Ma, if they had to rush to the air-raid shelter down the road. There had been drills all week. Everyone knew where they were supposed to go if the Japanese attacked.

Danny peeked around the blackout curtains on his window. Every house had to have these curtains. It had to be pitch dark at night so that the Japanese wouldn't see any targets from the sky. Danny hated being inside the sealed-up house. It made him think of being in a coffin, buried alive. It scared Danny.

Pretty much everything scared Danny.

You'd have to be crazy not to be scared, with what was happening in the world, with America at war with both Japan and Germany now. More troops were arriving every day at Pearl Harbor. Soon they'd all be sent to fight the Japanese in the Pacific, even Mack, who was almost well enough to start running bombing missions in his B-17. Danny knew Mack was sad to be leaving; he and Ma were good friends now. Danny never did have to make Ma go out to dinner with him. She asked him herself.

Danny was scared for Ma when she went to

take care of the men at Hickam. He was scared for Mr. Sudo, that he might get arrested again. He was scared that something bad could happen to Aki.

But, Danny decided, being scared was better than being numb.

If he were numb, he wouldn't be able to feel happy, and there were times when he caught himself smiling. Like when Mack came for dinner, or when Mr. Sudo was teaching him to draw, or when Aki rushed by with his crazy monkey smile, with no idea that so many bad things were happening.

And of course there was Finn.

Finn was better now. Danny found out because Ma had been allowed to use the phone at the hospital to call Mrs. Mills. Ma wanted her to spread the word in the neighborhood that she and Danny were safe. Mrs. Mills told her that Earl and all of his guys had enlisted in the army. And the most important news: Finn was out of the hospital, and he was staying with Mrs. Mills.

Danny liked the sound of that. He was writing Finn a long letter about what had happened to him during the attack. Ma said that all letters from Hawaii would be censored; soldiers would read his letter and cross out any information that could help the enemy. Danny didn't mind. He'd even asked Mr. Sudo to draw a picture of Aki for him to send. Mr. Sudo said that instead he would help Danny draw the picture. It was almost done. It wasn't good. But it didn't stink too bad.

Danny put his head back down on the pillow. At least the morning birds had come back. He liked to listen to them sing.

But then there was that strange sound again, the sound that had woken him up.

It sounded like a baby whimpering. Was Aki out there? He hadn't wandered since his father came home. But Danny wanted to make sure.

He threw on some clothes and went outside to the yard.

He followed the sound to one of the prickly bushes.

It wasn't Aki.

There, shaking like a leaf, was that baby wild boar, with the one white ear.

Danny looked around. Its mother monster was nowhere to be seen.

The baby was alone.

Danny picked it up.

The baby had changed in the past three weeks, like everything else.

Danny held it up and looked the little guy in the eye.

He looked scared. And tough. And like he'd be happy to have someone keep an eye on him.

Danny wasn't sure if it was possible to keep a wild boar as a pet. In fact, he was pretty sure it was a very bad idea.

But at that moment, Danny decided not to think about it — or anything else — as he headed up the hill to the Sudos' with the baby resting happily in his arms.

All he was thinking about was how Aki would smile when he saw his Christmas present.

PEARL HARBOR: A MAN-MADE DISASTER

Like all of the *I Survived* books, this book is a work of historical fiction. All of the main events and places are real. All of the characters come from my imagination.

But the tragic events of Pearl Harbor weren't caused by an iceberg or a storm or a hungry shark. The attack on Pearl Harbor was committed by men who plotted for months to cause as much destruction as possible. Why did Japan's leaders do this? What happened in the months and years after the attack? These are complicated questions, and I couldn't answer all of them in the story. So here is some more information, and suggestions for how you can explore this event further on your own.

Aaron Talshir

Why did the Japanese attack Pearl Harbor?

Today, the country of Japan is one of America's closest friends in the world. But in the 1930s, the relationship between the two countries was tense. Japan is a small country with few natural resources. At the time, Japan's leaders wanted more wealth and power. To achieve this, Japan's leaders began taking over lands that belonged to its neighboring countries, including China. Their plan was to build an empire, a collection of countries that Japan would control completely.

Japan's military leaders knew there was only one country on earth with the firepower to stop them: America. By bombing our ships and planes at Pearl Harbor, the Japanese believed they would—in a matter of hours—eliminate America as a threat.

How did America respond to the attacks?

The United States' first reaction was total shock. Few people ever imagined that Japan could seriously threaten America. Experts had under-estimated the skill of the Japanese military and the sophistication of their planes. In the first minutes of the attack, many people, even top military officers at Pearl Harbor, refused to believe that it was Japan dropping the bombs. Shock turned to horror, fear, and sadness. But then, very quickly, Americans became united and fiercely determined. The next day, Franklin D. Roosevelt appeared before our Congress and made a speech that is still one of the most famous in American history. He said that the date December 7th, 1941, would "live in infamy," meaning it would always be remembered as a day a great evil was committed. Thirty minutes later, America declared war on Japan. Millions of Americans rushed to join the military.

Our enemy was not only Japan, but Germany too. Those countries had made a secret agreement to fight together. America joined forces with England and France, which had been fighting against Germany since 1939. Our partnership with England and France, which eventually included Russia as well, became known as the "Allied forces." Japan joined Germany and Italy. Together they were known as the "Axis powers."

This fight became what we now call World War II. Between 1939 and 1945, the war raged throughout Europe and many small islands in the Pacific. It would become the bloodiest war in history; nearly 60 million people died, including more than 400,000 American soldiers. (In my imagination, Mack makes it back from his B-17 bombing runs alive to marry Danny's mom.)

After years of brutal fighting, America and the Allied forces finally won the war.

After the bombing of Pearl Harbor, what happened to Japanese people living in America?

In the hours after Pearl Harbor was attacked, the country of Japan became our bitter enemy. Many feared that the Japanese were planning to invade not only Hawaii, but also the West Coast of America. It was a frightening time in America, and for Japanese people living here, there were uniquely terrible challenges. Just four months after the Pearl Harbor attack, American leaders decided that Japanese people living in certain parts of the U.S. should be forced to live in special guarded camps far away from American cities. Entire families had to pack up, leave their homes and businesses, and move to these "internment camps." Approximately 100,000 people of Japanese descent, the majority of them American citizens, were forced to live in these guarded camps until the war ended in 1945. Today, the "internment" of loyal Japanese Americans is considered a shameful act in American history. The federal government officially apologized in 1983.

What is Pearl Harbor today?

Today, Pearl Harbor is still a major military base. It is also a monument and graveyard. If you go to Pearl Harbor, you can visit the USS *Arizona* Memorial. This is the final resting place for many of the sailors and marines who died when the ship exploded. It is also a beautiful monument where you can explore what happened that day.

The memorial is built over the sunken battleship, which rests in 40 feet of water at the bottom of the harbor. The ship still leaks drops of oil that rise to the surface of the water. I was lucky enough to visit this memorial. The drops of oil made me think of the tears that are still shed over the lives lost in the Pearl Harbor attack, and the sorrows of the long war that followed.

DEDICATED
TO THE ETERNAL MEMORY
OF OUR GALLANT SHIPMATES
IN THE USS ARIZONA
WHO GAVE THEIR LIVES IN ACTION
7 DECEMBER 1941

"FROM TODAY ON THE USS ARIZONA
WILL AGAIN FLY OUR COUNTRY'S FLAG
JUST AS PROUDLY AS SHE DID ON THE
MORNING OF 7 DECEMBER 1941.
I AM SURE THE ARIZONA'S CREW WILL
KNOW AND APPRECIATE WHAT WE ARE
DOING" ADMIRAL A.W. RADFORD, USN
7 MARCH 1950

MAY GOD MAKE HIS FACE
TO SHINE UPON THEM
AND GRANT THEM PEACE

PEARL HARBOR TIME LINE

What happened on the morning of December 7, 1941?

3:40 A.M. A U.S. ship called the *Condor* is patrolling the waters just two miles away from the entrance to Pearl Harbor. Members of the crew spot something in the water. They believe it is a small submarine, but they aren't sure. In fact, it is a Japanese "midget" submarine, one of five sent in advance of the attack. The *Condor* reports this to a nearby destroyer, the *Ward*.

6:10 A.M. In waters 235 miles north of Hawaii, Japanese planes take off from six aircraft carriers. The first

wave of planes includes 181 fighters,
bombers, and torpedo planes.

7:02 A.M. From a radar post not far
from Pearl Harbor, a radar operator
sees an alarming cluster of lights
on his screen. At least 50 planes
are heading from the north directly
toward Hawaii. He shows the officer
in charge, a man with little radar
experience. He mistakenly believes
the lights on the radar screen
are U.S. B-17 bombers returning
to their base from California.

7:15 A.M. The crew of the *Ward* finally
spots the submarine. They fire "depth
charge" explosives and sink the
sub. The crew of the *Ward* reports
this incident to Naval Headquarters
in Pearl Harbor, telling about the

sub. When Admiral Husband Kimmel
reads the message, he believes it
might be a false alarm and decides
to wait before taking action.

7:49 A.M. The first wave of Japanese
planes approaches Pearl Harbor.
The commander of the attack, Mitsuo
Fuchida, looks down on the quiet
morning and realizes that the Japanese
have achieved total surprise.

7:55 A.M. The attack begins as bombers
and torpedoes aim first for the seven
battleships. The *West Virginia* and
the *California* are hit and sink right
away, killing more than 200 men. The
Utah is hit and capsizes. The *Oklahoma*
is hit and rolls over, trapping
dozens of men; 32 will be rescued
after an agonizing 36-hour ordeal.

8:10 A.M. A powerful bomb explodes
through the deck of the *Arizona*,
igniting more than one million pounds
of gunpowder. The massive explosion
destroys the ship and instantly
kills 1,177 sailors and marines.

8:54 A.M. The second wave of 170
Japanese bombers arrives. This
time, they are met with anti-
aircraft fire. Bombs and torpedoes
hit ships throughout the harbor,
as well as planes and buildings
at the surrounding airfields.

10:00 A.M. The attack ends and
Japanese planes head back to their
aircraft carriers. The pilots
celebrate. The attack was a huge
success, but it was not complete. All
but three of the ships damaged in

the attack were eventually repaired
and sent back out to sea. America's
three Pacific aircraft carriers were,
by luck, not in the harbor that day
and escaped the attack completely.

MORE PEARL HARBOR FACTS:

- Number of American military
  personnel killed: 2,388

- Number of American civilians killed:
  48

- Number of Japanese military
  personnel killed: 64

- Number of ships sunk or beached: 12

- Number of ships damaged: 9

- Number of American aircraft
  destroyed: 164

TO FIND OUT MORE
ON YOUR OWN:

Here are some excellent books for kids I discovered during my research:

Remember Pearl Harbor, by Thomas B. Allen (National Geographic Books)

American and Japanese survivors tell their stories with great maps, charts, and timelines.

Attack on Pearl Harbor: The True Story of the Day America Entered World War II, by Shelley Tanaka, illustrated by David Craig (Madison Press Books)

The author shows how the attack affected three different people: a boy living in Hawaii, a sailor on the USS *Oklahoma*, and a Japanese pilot. There are also plenty of great pictures and other info.

Pearl Harbor Child, by Dorinda Makanaonalani Nicholson (Woodson House)

The author was a girl living in Pearl City when the attack happened.

The Children of Battleship Row: Pearl Harbor 1940–1941, by Joan Zuber Earl (RDR Books)

Joan's father was an admiral, and at the time of the attack her family lived on a little island right smack in the middle of the harbor. Her story makes you feel like you are there.

The National Geographic Society has a great Pearl Harbor website, with an amazing "attack map" and a time line that shows the attack minute by minute: **www.nationalgeographic. com/pearlharbor**.

What happens when a city on the rise suddenly falls?

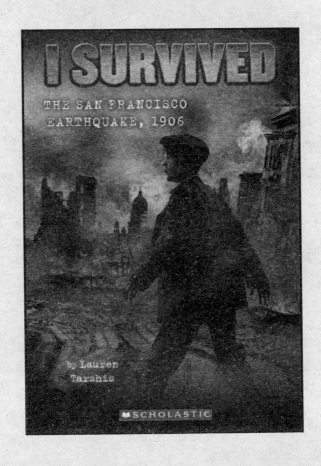

EVERYTHING CAME CRASHING DOWN...

Leo loves being a newsboy in San Francisco—the money he makes helps his family, and he's free to explore the amazing, hilly city as it grows with the new century. Horse-drawn carriages share the streets with shiny automobiles, businesses and families move in every day from everywhere, and anything seems possible.

But early one spring morning, everything changes. Leo's world is shaken—literally—and he finds himself stranded in the middle of San Francisco as it crumbles and burns to the ground. Does Leo have what it takes to survive this devastating disaster?

I SURVIVED

THE SINKING OF THE TITANIC, 1912

UNSINKABLE. UNTIL ONE NIGHT...

George Calder must be the luckiest kid alive. He and his little sister, Phoebe, are sailing with their aunt on the *Titanic*, the greatest ship ever built. George can't resist exploring every inch of the incredible boat, even if it keeps getting him into trouble.

Then the impossible happens—the *Titanic* hits an iceberg and water rushes in. George is stranded, alone and afraid, on the sinking ship. He's always gotten out of trouble before . . . but how can he survive this?

I SURVIVED

THE SHARK ATTACKS OF 1916

THERE'S SOMETHING IN THE WATER...

Chet Roscow is finally feeling at home in Elm Hills, New Jersey. He has a job with his uncle Jerry at the local diner, three great friends, and the perfect summertime destination: cool, refreshing Matawan Creek.

But Chet's summer is interrupted by shocking news. A great white shark has been attacking swimmers along the Jersey shore, not far from Elm Hills. Everyone in town is talking about it. So when Chet sees something in the creek, he's sure it's his imagination . . . until he comes face-to-face with a bloodthirsty shark!

I SURVIVED

HURRICANE KATRINA, 2005

HIS WHOLE WORLD IS UNDER WATER...

Barry's family tries to evacuate before Hurricane Katrina hits their home in the Lower Ninth Ward of New Orleans. But when Barry's little sister gets terribly sick, they're forced to stay home and wait out the storm.

At first, Katrina doesn't seem to be as severe a storm as forecasters predicted. But overnight the levees break, and Barry's world is literally torn apart. He's swept away by the floodwaters, away from his family. Can he survive the storm of the century — alone?